For Marco

A TEMPLAR BOOK
First published in the UK in 2005 by Templar Publishing,
an imprint of The Templar Company plc,
The Granary, North Street, Dorking, Surrey, RH4 1DN, UK
www.templarco.co.uk

3 5 7 9 10 8 6 4

ISBN: 978-1-84011-322-8

Designed by Andy Mansfield
Edited by Sue Harris

Printed in China

a goodnight warren book

Warren and the
Very Windy Day

Liane Payne

templar publishing

Warren the rabbit is very proud of his beautiful garden. He loves tending his flowers, humming and talking to them as he tidies and weeds. But sometimes he says, "I wish I had friends to share my garden with."

One morning, Warren is woken by a
tap-tap-tapping noise at the window.
He sleepily pulls back the curtain and sees
leaves whirling and swirling outside.
"What a very windy day!" he says.

Warren hurries outside and finds his beautiful tidy garden all messed up! The wind has whooshed everything round and round – his flowers have flopped over and his neat little lawn is littered with leaves. "Oh, bother!" says Warren.

Warren is very cross with the wind for making such a mess. Sighing, he starts sweeping the leaves into big piles.

He'd soon have his garden looking beautiful and tidy once more – just as it was before the wind ruined it...

But before Warren can pick up his
neat piles of leaves – WHOOSH! – A huge
gust of wind blows them all away again!
"I don't like the wind," grumbled Warren.

Warren was surprised when some little birds sang, "We LOVE the wind! It carried us here to spend the summer in your lovely garden. Then it will help us to fly home again before the cold winter comes!"

"Yes, but it still messed up my garden," muttered Warren, hurrying off to stake up his flowers.

Warren was still fussing about the wind when a passing butterfly said, "The wind's wonderful. It carries insects to your garden to gather nectar from your splendid flowers!" Warren smiled. His flowers were splendid, even after all the wind had done!

Warren was working hard to collect up all the leaves before the wind could blow them a way again, when a little voice said, "I like the wind, too. It swirls the leaves into mounds so I can make a cosy nest, and it blows the nuts off the trees for my winter food-store!" Warren looked behind the sack and found a mouse smiling up at him.

"The wind helps you, too, Warren," continued the mouse. "Look! It's blowing lots of interesting seeds into your garden. Next year, some of them will grow into lovely new plants."

Warren sat down and began to think. Perhaps the wind wasn't so bad after all. It seemed to be very useful. 'In fact,' he thought, 'the wind has made my wish come true – it's brought me lots of friends to share my garden with!'

That night, Warren and his new friend, Mouse, were tucked up in Warren's cosy sitting room, as the wind whistled and whooshed outside. Warren smiled. "I like the wind," he said, sleepily. Mouse nodded. "Me, too. It's a shame about the washing though…"

 "Goodnight, Warren!"

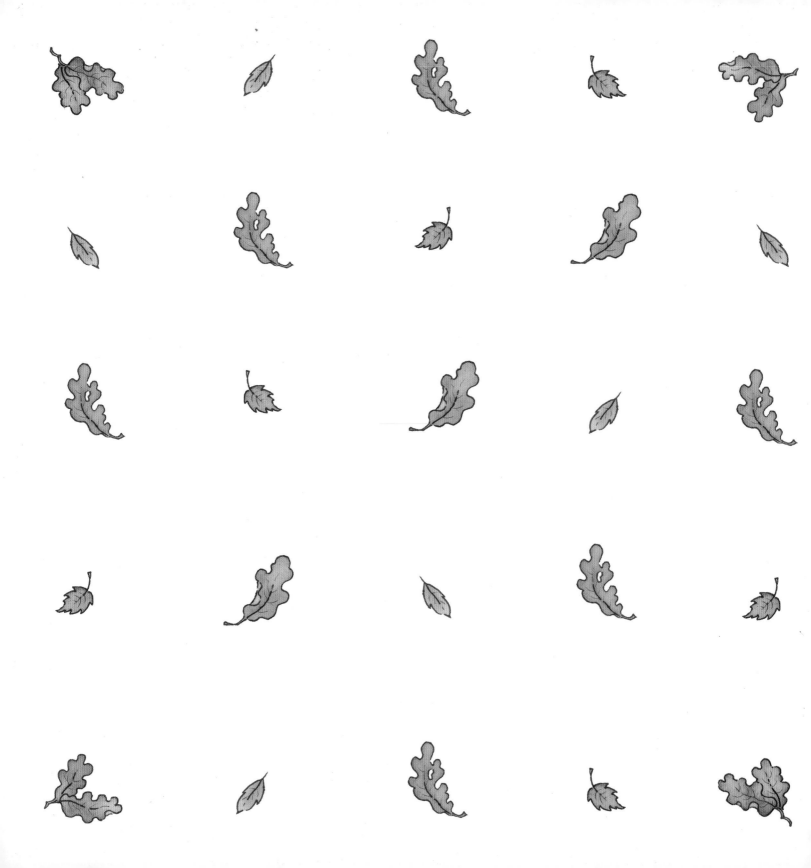